You Are Home
With Me

Sarah Asper-Smith

Illustrations by Mitchell Watley

little bigfoot
an imprint of sasquatch books
seattle, wa

For James Alexander—SAS and MW

Manufactured in China by C&C Offset Printing Co. Ltd. Shenzhen,
Guangdong Province, in June 2019

Published by Little Bigfoot, an imprint of Sasquatch Books

LITTLE BIGFOOT with colophon is a registered trademark of
Penguin Random House LLC

23 22 21 20 19   9 8 7 6 5 4 3 2 1

Editor: Christy Cox | Production editor: Jill Saginario
Design: Bryce de Flamand

Library of Congress Cataloging-in-Publication Data

Names: Asper-Smith, Sarah, author. | Watley, Mitchell, illustrator.
Title: You are home with me / Sarah Asper-Smith ; illustrated by
   Mitchell Watley.
Description: Seattle, WA : Little Bigfoot, an imprint of Sasquatch Books,
   [2019] | Summary: Intersperses facts about different animals and birds
   with reassurances that a parent would take care of a child and make a
   home for him or her, no matter what.
Identifiers: LCCN 2018054673 | ISBN 9781632172242 (hard cover)
Subjects: | CYAC: Parent and child--Fiction. | Parental behavior in
   animals--Fiction. | Animals--Habitations--Fiction. | Habitat
   (Ecology)--Fiction.
Classification: LCC PZ7.A8405 You 2019 | DDC [E]--dc23
LC record available at https://lccn.loc.gov/2018054673

ISBN: 978-1-63217-224-2

Sasquatch Books
1904 Third Avenue, Suite 710
Seattle, WA 98101
SasquatchBooks.com

If you were a **raven**, we would live in a tree high above the ground in a nest of woven branches and twigs.

Ravens are playful; they somersault in the sky and slide down hills in the snow.

Polar bears have black
skin under their fur to
soak up the sun's rays
and keep them warm.

If you were a **polar bear**, I would carve out a den in a snowbank to keep you warm and safe.

The blue whale is the largest animal on earth and one of the loudest! They can be heard up to one thousand miles away.

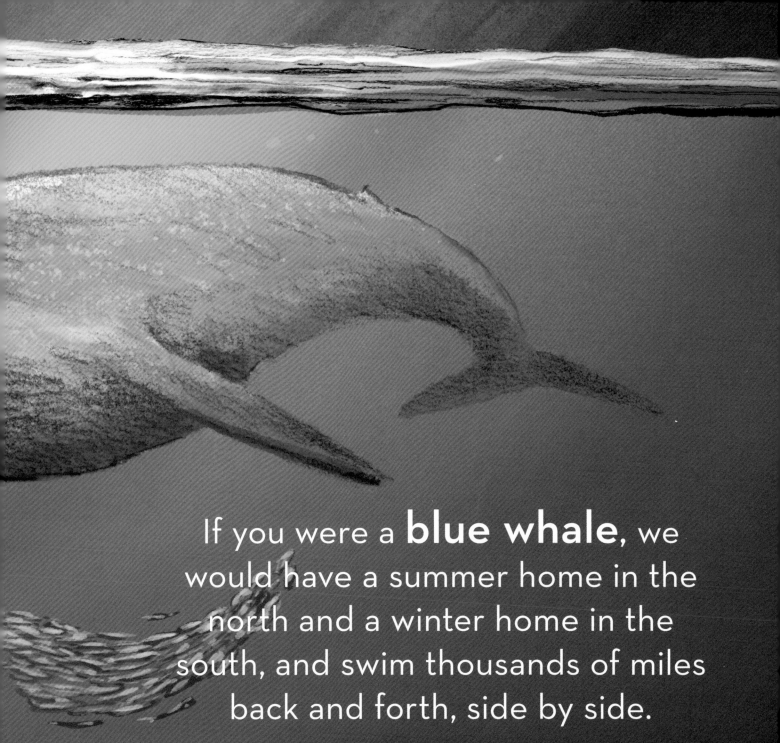

If you were a **blue whale**, we would have a summer home in the north and a winter home in the south, and swim thousands of miles back and forth, side by side.

If you were a **mountain goat**, we would scramble up and down mountain cliffs, and leap from rock to rock together.

You can tell the age of a mountain goat by counting the rings on its horns.

If you were a **flying squirrel**, we would live in a hole within a tree, and glide together through the forest at night.

Flying squirrels don't actually fly,
but glide from tree to tree with
their arms and legs outstretched.

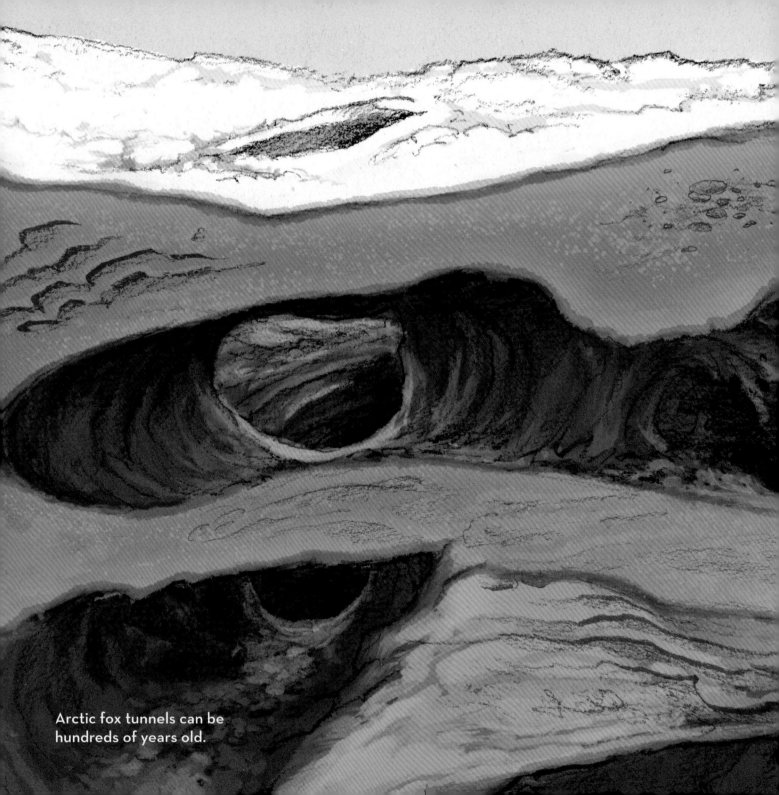

Arctic fox tunnels can be
hundreds of years old.

If you were an **arctic fox**, we would explore for miles in our tunnels and dens below the ice and snow.

If you were a **tufted puffin**, I would dig a burrow to shelter you on the edge of a cliff near the sea.

Tufted puffins have sharp nails on their feet to help them climb over rocks.

Dall's porpoises are very fast swimmers,
reaching speeds of thirty-four miles per hour.

If you were a **Dall's porpoise**,
we would dive down deep in our ocean
home, and swim back to the surface
to jump and play in the waves.

Lynx kittens stay with their mother for the first year to learn to hunt.

If you were a **lynx**, I would search for a fallen tree to shelter us, and we would snuggle behind the roots to stay warm.

Hoary marmots make many sounds.
They can chirp, growl, whine, and whistle.

If you were a **hoary marmot**, I would whistle to warn you of danger and keep you safe in our burrow high up in the mountains.

If you were a **moose**, we would find a new place to sleep every night, stomping down the ground in a circle to form a bed.

Moose calves are able to swim as soon as two weeks after they're born.

If you were a **tundra swan**, I would protect you in a nest made of moss and grass on the Arctic tundra.

Tundra swans sleep on land with their young,
but in the winter they migrate south and sleep on water.

Sea lions use their back flippers to walk on land.

If you were a **sea lion**, we would live in the ocean and haul out on a rock together to be warmed by the sun.

If you were a **beaver**, I would gnaw on trees with my teeth to build a cozy lodge for us to sleep in during the day.

Beavers have transparent eyelids
to help them see under water.

Gray wolves live in packs and communicate with each other through growls, barks, whines, howls, and body language.

If you were a **gray wolf**, all of the members of our pack would share our den, and they would help take care of you.

Wherever you may be, you will always have a home with me.